For Danni Corgan – J.W.

American edition published in 2021 by Andersen Press USA,
an imprint of Andersen Press Ltd.
www.andersenpressusa.com

First published in Great Britain in 2021 by Andersen Press Ltd.,
20 Vauxhall Bridge Road, London SW1V 2SA.

Text copyright © Jeanne Willis
Illustration copyright © Tony Ross

Distributed in the United States and Canada by
Lerner Publishing Group, Inc.
241 First Avenue North
Minneapolis, MN 55401 USA

For reading levels and more information, look up this title at www.lernerbooks.com.

Printed and bound in China

Library of Congress Cataloging-in-Publication Data Available
ISBN: 978-1-72842-412-5

1 – TWP – 9/2020

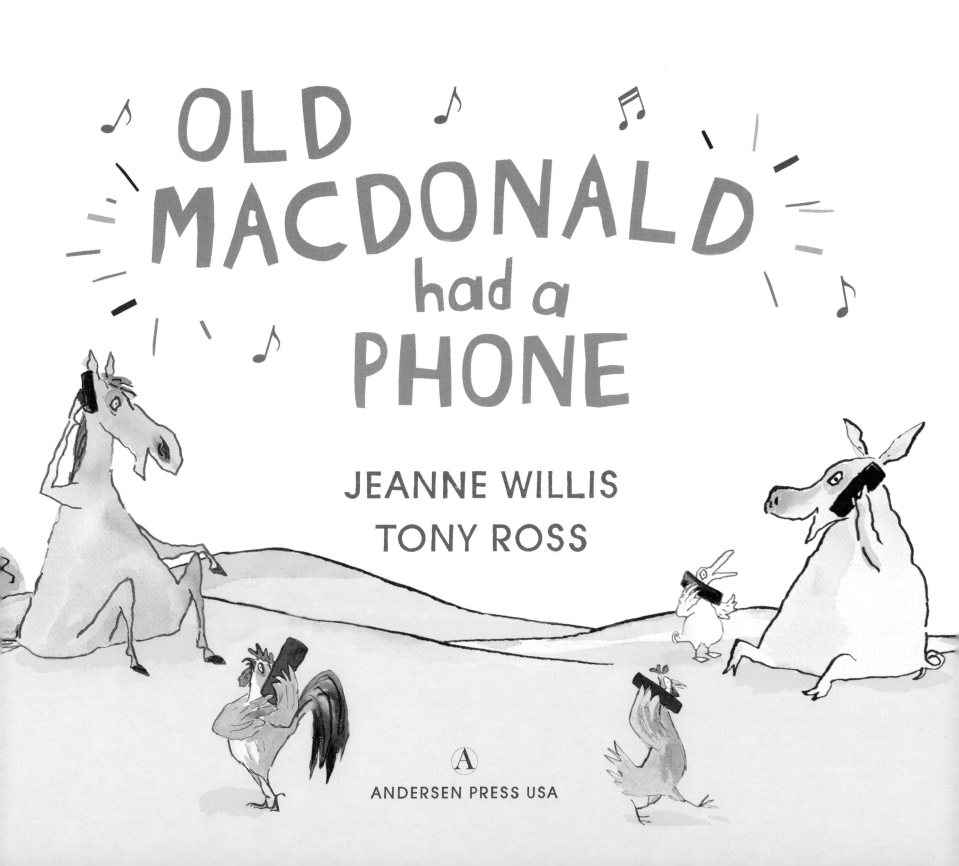

OLD MACDONALD had a PHONE

JEANNE WILLIS

TONY ROSS

ANDERSEN PRESS USA

♫ ♪ Old Macdonald had a phone ♫ ♪

And it was very smart,

It helped him organize his farm
And fill his shopping cart . . .

♪ With a tractor here ♪
And a pig trough there,

Chicken feed, cabbage seed,
Everything that he might need.

♫ Old Macdonald had a phone ♪

He dropped it in the lake.

He ordered one online but . . .

Bought a hundred by mistake!

They were taken by the cows,
The boars and the sows,
The rooster, sheep, and hens,
And all their furry friends.

♪ ♪ Everybody had a phone ♫
And it was such good fun!

Nobody would put them down
So nothing else got done.

The rooster didn't crow,

The horse wouldn't go ...

The sheep ignored the rams,
The sheepdog lost the lambs.

Old Macdonald had a farm
But nothing in his shop,

Cows messaging at milking time
Would not produce a drop.

♪ The hens wouldn't lay, ♫
On their phones all day,

Here a tweet, there a chat,
WhatsApping the farm cat.

♪ Old Macdonald used to run ♪
The noisiest of farms,
Now all he hears are ringtones
And the beep of phone alarms.

Old Macdonald took the phones
And locked them in the shed,
It made the sheepdog so annoyed,
He sulked and went to bed.

The fox scared the sheep,

The rooster stayed asleep,

The bull refused to sweep
His manure in a heap . . .

Young Macdonald found his dad
Sobbing in his van,
"Smart phones aren't
so bad," he said.
"Get with the times, old man."

"Like all technology,
If we use it sensibly
And live life to the full,
Then phones are cool."

They had a meeting at the farm
With all the animals,
And promised to give back the phones
If they obeyed these rules:
A chat-chat here, and a selfie there,
But not all day! Does that sound fair?

♪ The creatures at Macdonald's Farm ♫
Agreed with what was said.
They limited their phone time,
And they ran the farm instead.

♪ The eggs were laid, ♪

The milk was made . . .

They all had a party
Now the bills were paid!

♪ ♪ All the creatures on the farm ♪♪
Are happy as can be,
They talk to one another
And they do not text at tea.

♫ Rooster crows at dawn, ♪
The sheep are shorn . . .

Lots of little pigs

And lambs are born . . .

♫ Best of all, Macdonald's bull ♪
Won first prize in the show,

And everybody texted . . .

Smiley Face, YOLO! YOLO!